Karen's Swim Meet

**Other books by
Ann M. Martin**

P. S. Longer Letter Later
(written with Paula Danziger)
Leo the Magnificat
Rachel Parker, Kindergarten Show-off
Eleven Kids, One Summer
Ma and Pa Dracula
Yours Turly, Shirley
Ten Kids, No Pets
With You and Without You
Me and Katie (the Pest)
Stage Fright
Inside Out
Bummer Summer

For older readers:

Missing Since Monday
Just a Summer Romance
Slam Book

Little Sister

Karen's Swim Meet
Ann M. Martin

Illustrations by Susan Crocca Tang

A
LITTLE APPLE
PAPERBACK

SCHOLASTIC INC.
New York Toronto London Auckland Sydney
Mexico City New Delhi Hong Kong

ISBN 0-590-50062-7

12 11 10 9 8 7 6 5 4 3 2 1   9/9 0 1 2 3 4/0

Printed in the U.S.A.   40
First Scholastic printing, June 1999

The author gratefully acknowledges
Stephanie Calmenson
for her help
with this book.

A Surprise to Come

"Watch out, Karen!" said Hannie. "It is about to drip!"

I twirled my strawberry Popsicle around and licked the bottom just in time.

Then Nancy had to make an emergency rescue on hers. "These Popsicles are dripping really fast," she said between slurps.

"That is because it is so hot out," I replied.

It was unusually hot for a June day. Even sitting under a shady tree in the big-house backyard did not help much.

Wait. You do not know about my big

house yet. I will tell you about that later. More important, you do not know about me yet. I will tell you about me right now.

My name is Karen Brewer. I have blonde hair, blue eyes, and freckles. (By the end of the summer, I will have a lot more freckles than I have now.) I am seven years old and wear glasses. I have two pairs. I wear the blue pair for reading. I wear the pink pair the rest of the time.

My two best friends are Hannie Papadakis and Nancy Dawes. We call ourselves the Three Musketeers. That is because we like to do everything together. I was happy we were together on the first day of our summer vacation.

"We have to think of exciting things to do this summer," I said when we finished our Popsicles.

"I will have to wait until July," said Hannie. "I just found out I am going on vacation with my family. We were on a waiting list for a cabin in the mountains and we got called last night. They have a cabin for us, so we are leaving the day after tomorrow."

"I will have to wait too," said Nancy. "I am not going away. But I will be very busy with my family. My cousins from Minnesota said they wanted to visit this summer. They are driving and will be here any day."

I was surprised to hear this news from my friends. This was not a good surprise. It made me feel grouchy.

"Boo," I said. "Now I have to think of something exciting to do all by myself."

"I am sorry," said Hannie.

"Me too," said Nancy. "But it is only for a couple of weeks. We can do something exciting together in July."

"Can we do something together on the Fourth of July?" I asked.

Both my friends said yes.

"Great!" I said. "I will plan a Fourth of July surprise for us!"

I was finished being grouchy. (I never stay grouchy very long.)

"What kind of surprise?" asked Hannie.

"If I tell you, it will not be a surprise anymore," I replied. "But I promise it will be worth coming home for."

"I will be coming home anyway. But it is nice to have something to look forward to," said Hannie.

Just then a car pulled into the driveway. It was Nancy's mother. She was going to drive Nancy home. Nancy's house is right next door to my little house.

Oh. I have not told you about my houses. I will do that now.

Big-House Barbecue

Hannie went home after Nancy did. (She lives across the street and one house over from the big house.) I was alone in the yard. It was late in the afternoon and starting to cool off. I decided that under the tree in my big-house backyard was just the right place to be. I sat there thinking about my two yards, two houses, two families.

I did not always have two families. I used to have just one. That was a long time ago when I was little. Then my family was Mommy, Daddy, Andrew, and me. (Andrew is my little brother. He is four going on five.) We all lived together here in the big house in Stoneybrook, Connecticut.

Then things started changing. Mommy and Daddy were having trouble getting along. They argued all the time. They tried hard to work things out. But they just could not do it. They told Andrew and me that they loved us very much and always would. But they did not want to live with each other anymore.

So Mommy and Daddy got divorced. Mommy moved with Andrew and me to a little house not far away. She met a very nice man named Seth Engle. She and Seth got married and now Seth is my stepfather.

That means there are four of us at the little house when we are all together. We also have some pets. They are Emily Junior, my rat; Bob, Andrew's hermit crab; Midgie, Seth's dog; and Rocky, Seth's cat.

Daddy stayed in the big house after he and Mommy got divorced. (It is the house he grew up in.) He met and married Elizabeth Thomas and now Elizabeth is my stepmother. She is really nice too. Elizabeth was married once before and has four children. They are my stepbrothers and stepsister. They are David Michael, who is seven like me; Kristy, who is thirteen and the best stepsister ever; and Sam and Charlie, who are so old they are in high school.

I also have a little sister, Emily Michelle, who is two and a half. I love her a lot, which is why I named my rat after her. Daddy and Elizabeth adopted her from a faraway country called Vietnam.

The other person living at the big house is Nannie. She is Elizabeth's mother, which makes her my stepgrandmother. She came to live at the big house to help with Emily. But she helps everyone.

We have pets at the big house too. Lots of them. They are Shannon, David Michael's big Bernese mountain dog puppy; Pumpkin, our little black kitten; Crystal Light the Second, my goldfish; and Goldfishie, Andrew's flamingo. (Just kidding!) Emily Junior and Bob live at the big house whenever Andrew and I are there.

Andrew and I switch houses almost every month. We spend one month at the big house, then one month at the little house. I gave my brother and me special names. I call us Andrew Two-Two and Karen Two-Two. (I thought of those names after my teacher read a book to our class. It was called *Jacob Two-Two Meets the Hooded Fang*.) I call us those names because we each have two of so many things. We have two families with two mommies and two daddies. We have two sets of toys and clothes and books. We have two bicycles, one at each house. And you already know about my two best friends, Hannie and Nancy. The three of us are in the same second-grade class at Stoneybrook Academy. We have a wonderful teacher named Ms. Colman.

I was thinking about my two families when I heard Elizabeth call my name.

"Karen, would you like to come help us? We are going to have a barbecue tonight," she said.

I jumped up. I love barbecues! Especially big-house barbecues.

"I am on my way!" I replied.

My favorite barbecue job is helping with the corn. There are ten of us, so we buy two dozen ears. That meant I had a lot of work ahead of me. I was ready for it.

Swim Team

Our barbecue was delicious. Nannie had to remind me to stop eating. The last time we barbecued, I ate so much I got a bellyache.

I was listening to everyone talking about their summer plans. I would have been talking about my summer plans, only I did not have any. Then I heard something interesting.

"Ron Carson is back in town," said Charlie. "I hear he is opening a sports store and will be coaching a swim team."

"I know who Ron Carson is!" I said. "Ms. Colman was friends with him in high school. He is a swimming star."

"He sure is," said Sam. "He was so good that he made it all the way to the Olympic trials. Some of his trophies are on display at the pool."

"I bet you have to be a really good swimmer to join his team," I said.

"That is not what I read in the paper," said Daddy. "It said kids of all ages are welcome to join. They can be good swimmers or beginners."

Hmm. I am a pretty good swimmer. Maybe I was going to have a summer plan after all. I felt a little nervous about joining without my friends. But I did not want to stay home and do nothing.

"Can we call tomorrow to find out about joining?" I asked.

"I will call first thing in the morning," said Elizabeth.

*   *   *

When I came downstairs to breakfast the next morning, Elizabeth was already on the phone.

I came downstairs late because I had stayed in bed reading. I was reading a very good summertime book called *Half Magic*. It is about four kids who had nothing to do over the summer. Then one of them found a magic coin. I did not think I was going to find a magic coin in Stoneybrook. I hoped I could join the swim team instead.

"Yes, Mr. Carson, I have the hours all written down," said Elizabeth. "Thank you for the information."

"You talked to Ron Carson himself?" I said when she hung up the phone. "That is exciting! Was he nice? Does he want me on the team?"

"He sounded very nice. And he wants anyone interested in swimming to sign up," Elizabeth replied.

Elizabeth told me that practices for my age group would be held every weekday morning at nine, before the pool opened to the public. That meant no more early-morning reading in bed. But that was okay. I would still have plenty of time left over to do what I wanted after practice.

I took a deep breath. I was still a little nervous about signing up without knowing anyone. But being on a swim team with a famous coach sounded gigundoly cool. So I decided to be brave.

"How do I sign up?" I asked.

"All I have to do is call Mr. Carson back and tell him to add your name to his list," Elizabeth replied.

"Go for it!" said Charlie, walking into the kitchen.

"All right," I said. "Sign me up. Tell Mr. Carson that Karen Brewer is on the team!"

Dive Right In!

On Monday morning Daddy took me to the pool early. We arrived at ten to nine. I was nervous, so I had a little talk with myself.

"You can do this, Karen Brewer," I said. "You can join this team all by yourself."

While I was talking to myself, another car pulled up. Terri Barkan stepped out.

"Hi, Terri!" I said. "Are you going to be on the team? I did not know you were a swimmer."

"I am not very good. But I needed something to do in the mornings because my mom started a new job. Plus, I thought being on the team would help me swim better," said Terri.

"Where is Tammy?" I asked.

"She is taking tennis lessons," Terri replied.

Terri and her twin sister, Tammy, are in my class at school. They are very nice.

It was easy saying good-bye to Daddy with Terri there. We walked to the pool together. Coach Carson was standing by the diving board. A whistle was hanging from his neck and a clipboard was in his hand. He got started right away.

"I want to give you the ground rules for the team," he said. "Practice begins at nine o'clock sharp every weekday morning. Meets will be held in the evenings, one or two nights a week. We will compete against teams from neighboring towns. Please encourage your parents to come."

Terri and I looked at each other. Mr. Carson seemed like a very serious person. I wished he would smile or make a joke or something. But he did not.

"I had my first real swimming lessons at summer camp," he said. "As soon as I learned to swim properly, they could not keep me out of the water. I am a very competitive person and always do my best when someone is trying to beat me. I want to teach you to swim right and swim to win."

Then he taught us a cheer to get us in the mood for our workout.

When Coach blows the whistle, we are ready to swim.
When Coach blows the whistle, we will dive right in.
Backstroke, breaststroke, butterfly, crawl.
When Coach blows the whistle, we will do them all!

"Okay, kids! Get ready for the freestyle," called Coach Carson.

I took off my shorts and T-shirt. Then I

stuffed my hair in my cap and put on my goggles. I already knew that freestyle and crawl are two names for the same stroke. I am good at it.

"Swim next to me," whispered Terri.

I stood in the lane next to Terri's and waited for the starting whistle.

"Fifteen seconds to go," called our coach.

The whistle blew. I swam up the lane, then back. Up the lane, then back. I listened for the whistle again. But I did not hear it. I kept going. Up the lane, then back. I was swimming a long time and did not hear the whistle. I thought maybe I had water in my ears and could not hear it. But everyone else was still swimming too. Up the lane, then back. I swam back and forth so many times I lost count. Finally the whistle blew.

Terri was the last one to reach the wall again. She was huffing and puffing.

"We will rest for thirty seconds, then do the backstroke," said Coach Carson.

Terri looked at me and made a face. I did

not have a chance to say anything before the whistle blew again.

I am not very good at the backstroke. But I could keep up. We swam for a long time again. Then we did the breaststroke. Then we used kickboards. Finally practice was over.

"See you tomorrow. Nine o'clock sharp. Go, team, go!" said Coach Carson.

I was tired but excited about swimming.

"This was fun!" I said to Terri.

She did not think so. She looked at me and rolled her eyes.

Water Wings

"Backstroke, breaststroke, butterfly, crawl! When Coach blows the whistle, we will do them all! Yea!"

I had recited the cheer for Daddy when he came to pick me up. Now I was reciting it again for Elizabeth, Nannie, and Emily. (Daddy and Elizabeth were taking Mondays and Fridays off from work over the summer.)

"I guess that cheer means you enjoyed your swim practice," said Nannie. "I am glad to hear it."

"I remember when Ron Carson was winning swim meets for Stoneybrook years ago," said Elizabeth. "He made our town proud."

"Getting to the Olympic trials was quite an accomplishment," replied Daddy. "Ron had to compete against the best swimmers in the country."

"And now he is *my* coach!" I said. "I am a lucky swimmer."

"Speaking of swimming, who would like to go for a swim in the Kormans' pool?" asked Nannie. "It is very hot out."

"Good idea," said Daddy. "It was nice of the Kormans to invite us to use their pool while they are away. We should take advantage of it."

We all went inside to get our bathing suits. Nannie made sure I hung up my wet one from practice. Then she gave me cookies and lemonade.

"You must be hungry after all your swimming," she said.

"I am!" I replied.

Soon everyone was downstairs and ready to go.

"I have sunscreen. And I have water wings for Emily," said Elizabeth when she came downstairs.

"I have towels and some fruit," said Nannie.

"And I have Emily!" I said, holding up my little sister's hand.

Daddy held Emily's other hand and we walked across the street together. (The Kormans' house is two houses down from Hannie's. I waved to Hannie's house as I went by.)

We did not waste a minute when we reached their house. We got right into the pool. Elizabeth carried Emily in her arms.

I was paddling around them in circles when Emily started calling, "Emmie swim! Emmie fish!"

She started kicking her legs and waving her arms.

"I would like you to be a fish with water wings," said Daddy.

He put them on Emily's arms. Elizabeth took her by the hands and pulled her around the shallow end of the pool. Emily was kicking her legs like a real swimmer.

When Elizabeth stopped pulling her, Emily cried, "More! Swim more!"

"Emily, you really are swimming!" I said.

Usually when we go in the water, Emily is happy just to be in Elizabeth's arms. This was the first time I had seen her try to swim on her own.

She could not get enough of it. We stayed at the pool for a long time.

At dinner I told everyone about practice and Ron Carson. Emily told everyone she was a fish.

"Emmie swim! Emmie fish!" she announced.

At bedtime, Emily was so excited she could not get to sleep. Elizabeth and I took turns reading *One Fish, Two Fish, Red Fish, Blue Fish* to her. We had to read it six times.

I had trouble falling asleep too. I started thinking about swim practice and Coach

Carson and Terri Barkan. Then I closed my eyes and pictured myself swimming back and forth in the water. Back and forth. Back and forth.

That did it. The next thing I knew it was morning.

A New Friend

At breakfast Sam said, "Look who is in the newspaper, Karen. Ron Carson. It tells how he grew up here in town. And it lists all the medals he has won."

"Let me see, please!" I said.

I was gigundoly proud to have a superstar coach. Maybe he would help me turn into a superstar swimmer. I would swim laps faster than anyone. The coach would recommend me for the Olympic trials. There would be articles about me in the newspaper: "Karen Brewer, New Stoneybrook Swim Star." My trophies would be on display at the pool. Then I, Karen Brewer, would take over Coach Carson's job when he retired.

"Come on, Karen," said Daddy. "It is time to go."

Oops. I was so busy dreaming, I had stopped eating my breakfast. I stuffed a chunk of banana in my mouth and jumped up. I did not want to be late. We pulled up to the Community Center just as Terri and her mom did.

"Yesterday was hard work," said Terri. "I hope today will be a little easier."

As soon as we were ready, the coach blew his whistle.

"Good morning, swimmers!" he said. "Before our workout, I want to get your orders for our team T-shirts."

"Yes!" I said to Terri.

We lined up to give the coach our orders. When it was my turn, I made sure to tell him that I knew Ms. Colman. I was excited that a town hero and I knew the same person.

"I am sure she is an excellent teacher," said Coach Carson. "Name and size, please."

He did not seem to care that I knew Ms. Colman. After taking our orders, he asked us to line up at the pool.

Terri was on my left. A girl I did not know was on my right. She was bouncing up and down, shaking out her hands. I could tell she could not wait to get in the water.

I wanted to introduce myself, but I did not have a chance. The coach was giving us instructions. We had to swim twelve laps. Two freestyle, two backstroke, two breaststroke. Then do it again without stopping.

I heard Terri sigh. Then the whistle blew. There was a big splash on my right. I did not know why. I did not have time to think about it. I had to swim!

I reached the wall just before the end-of-the-round whistle. The new girl was already there. Terri was all the way at the other end of the pool.

"I did only ten laps," she gasped when she finally reached the wall.

Coach Carson spent some time working with us on our strokes. He showed us how they should be done. Then he walked around and gave us each pointers.

He was just finishing when someone from the Community Center came out to speak with him.

"You can have free swim while I am talking," he said.

The girl in the next lane smiled at me.

"Hi," I said. "I am Karen. This is Terri."

"I am Kristin. I am here for the summer visiting my aunt," said the girl. "Do you want to race me across?"

"Okay!" I said.

Terri said she did not want to race. But she started us off.

"On your mark, get set, go!"

I swam hard, but Kristin won. I did not mind. I had fun.

Kristin, Terri, and I had a splashing contest. We all won! Then Coach Carson blew the whistle. It was time to go back to our practice. The second day was even better than the first. At the end, Coach Carson led us in a new cheer.

"This will be the cheer for our meets," he said.

Two, four, six, eight,
We are Stoneybrook swimmers and we are
  great!
We are Stoneybrook swimmers and we are
  cool.
Better watch out when we jump in the pool!

Terri, Kristin, and I were the best cheerers on the team. I was happy to be making new friends. (I had not spent much time with Terri outside of school before.)

As we were leaving, Terri said, "I know I need some extra help. Maybe the coach will give me one-on-one lessons."

I had an idea. Kristin and I were better

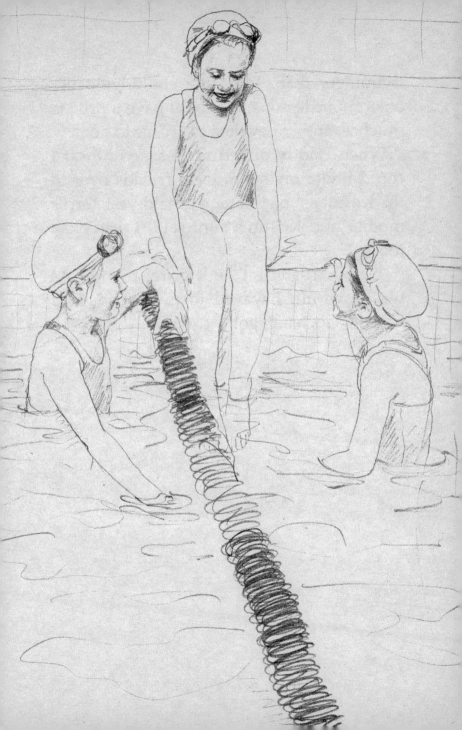

swimmers than Terri. We could give her one-on-one lessons. We could have a private practice, and I knew just the place to do it.

When Daddy pulled up, I asked him if I could invite my swim team friends over to the Kormans' pool later. He said yes! Terri's mother and Kristin's aunt said it was okay too.

"See you later!" I said to my friends. As we drove off, I waved to my friends and called, "Go, team, go!"

Kristin's Secret

At five o'clock that afternoon, Terri, Kristin, Daddy, Emily, and I walked to the Kormans' pool.

Daddy watched us while he helped Emily paddle around.

"I think you need to pull your knees up more when you do the frog kick," I said to Terri.

The frog kick is part of the breaststroke.

"Hang on to the side of the pool and kick. I will go underwater and watch," said Kristin.

Kristin ducked under while Terri kicked. She seemed to be under a long time. Finally she came up.

"How did I do?" asked Terri.

"Okay, I think," said Kristin. "I am not really sure. I know how to do it, but I do not know what it is supposed to look like."

"We can ask Coach Carson at the next practice," I said. "Now we should show Terri the freestyle stroke."

Kristin and I walked around to the deep end. In no time Kristin was in the water. She jumped up, grabbed her knees, then dropped into the pool with a big splash.

"What is that called?" I asked.

"It is called a cannonball," said Kristin. "That is how I get in the water."

"You go farther if you dive in," I said. "Watch this."

I got out of the pool. Then I dove back in, glided, and came up a few feet from the wall.

"See?" I said.

"Yes, but I do not like to go in headfirst," said Kristin.

"Why not? Even I can do that," said Terri.

She climbed out, then dove back into the water.

"I cannot do it," said Kristin. "I mean I can. I just do not want to. I am scared."

"Really? But you are such a good swimmer," said Terri.

"I am good once I get into the water," Kristin replied. "But going in the water headfirst is too scary for me. I hope I can swim backstroke at our meets. You start off in the water, and do not have to dive in."

"Well, now that we are all in, we should show Terri the freestyle stroke," I said.

I swam across the pool first. Kristin followed me.

"Your turn!" we called to Terri.

I could see a couple of things Terri was doing to slow herself down. She was lifting her head too high when she breathed. She was swinging her arms way out. I hoped Coach Carson would be able to work with her. For now, Kristin and I tried our best.

"I do not know if I improved much, but I sure feel better about my swimming," said Terri. "Thank you!"

When we finished with our lesson, we all tried doing flip turns against the side of the pool. The swimmers on TV make them look so easy.

"Ouch!" I said. "I keep hitting the wall."

"You have to turn sooner," said Kristin. "Only not too soon or you will miss the wall completely. Like me."

Then we started fooling around in the water. That is something we all did perfectly!

"Watch this!" said Terri.

She did a handstand in the water. Emily started to clap. She was watching everything we did.

"It is time to go, girls," said Daddy.

I was glad Kristin and Terri were staying for dinner. We were having lots of fun. Then I remembered something I was supposed to be doing. I was supposed to be planning a Fourth of July surprise for Hannie and

Nancy. I decided that planning the surprise would be much more fun with my new friends. And I wanted them to be part of it.

"I have some planning to do. I need your help," I told Kristin and Terri as we walked back to my house. "And whatever the plan is, you are invited."

Three Good Friends

The next day at the start of practice, Coach Carson announced that our first meet would be on Thursday night.

"So we need to get serious," said the coach. "We do not want to let Stoneybrook down."

He divided us into lanes by our speeds. Swimmers who were the same speed shared a lane.

I was in a lane with Kristin, even though she swims a little faster than I do. Terri was in the slower lane next to ours. We could still talk to one another, though.

"Ten seconds till the first round," called Coach Carson. "And I have seen at least one of you getting into the pool with a cannonball. I do not want to see that again."

I glanced at Kristin. She looked upset.

"That is okay," I said. "You do not have to dive in headfirst. You can just slip in quietly. He did not say anything about slipping into the pool."

Two seconds later, the whistle blew. We were doing our start-up rounds: two freestyle, two backstroke, two breaststroke. There was a big clock by the pool and I noticed I was getting a little faster with each lap. The coach was giving excellent pointers. I only wished he had time to give us some more. Especially Terri.

The coach blew the end-of-the-round whistle.

"Now I am going to help some swimmers individually," he said. "The rest of you do warm-up exercises."

"Great! Maybe now I will get some help. I need it for the meet," said Terri.

But Coach Carson did not come anywhere near us. He was bending down and talking to the faster kids, who were working on shaving seconds off their times.

"I am sure he will come to us later," said Kristin. "We *all* need help with the breast-stroke kick."

While we waited we kept warm doing a water ballet. I lifted my leg as high as I could and pointed my toes in the air. My friends did the same thing. Then we twirled around so many times we got dizzy.

"It is a good thing we are in the water. It will not hurt when we fall," said Terri.

She made believe she was fainting and dove under the water. She swam in circles between Kristin and me.

"We need water ballet costumes," I said. "Our bathing suits should have little skirts on them."

"We do not need ballet skirts," said

Kristin. "But we do need matching outfits for the meet."

"We can wear matching caps and suits," said Terri. "Who has a red suit?"

"I have blue," I replied. "Who has blue?"

"I do!" said Terri.

"So do I," said Kristin. "And we can wear red caps."

The coach never did come over to us. But we forgot all about that. We were having too much fun.

Before we left, we signed up to swim the relay race at the meet. Terri, Kristin, and I were not exactly the Three Musketeers. But we were becoming three good friends.

An Exciting Plan

"Only Emmie!" called my sister.

"I would like to go in the pool with you," said Nannie.

"No," said Emily. She started to pout.

Nannie, Emily, and I were at the Kormans' pool. Emily wanted to go swimming all by herself. She was doing very well with her water wings, but Nannie could not let her go in the water alone. Emily was too little.

"I will sit on the steps," said Nannie.

Emily looked as though she were going to cry. Then I had an idea.

"Can I go in the pool?" I asked. "I need to practice my swimming."

I could not really practice my swimming in the shallow end. But Emily did not know that.

"Okay!" said Emily.

Nannie mouthed the words "Thank you" to me. I got in the pool and stood by Emily as she paddled around.

"Do you want to be a boat?" I asked Emily.

"Emmie be Little Toot!" she replied.

Little Toot is a book about a boat that Emily likes us to read to her.

"Okay, Little Toot," I said. "Get ready to sail."

I pulled Emily around in circles. She threw her head back and laughed.

Emily and I were having lots of fun at the Kormans' pool. The day before, I had had fun at the pool with Terri and Kristin. That gave me an idea.

"Nannie, I promised Hannie and Nancy I would plan a surprise for them on the Fourth of July. Do you think we could have a picnic here at the pool?" I asked.

"I cannot give you permission until we ask the Kormans," replied Nannie. "But I do not think they would mind. I will leave a message on their answering machine."

"Thank you!" I said.

Nannie called the Kormans as soon as we got home. She asked if it would be all right for me to invite a small group of my friends for a picnic at their pool.

Before they left on vacation, the Kormans had said they would check their messages every evening. I hoped they would get back to us right away.

After dinner, the phone rang. I raced to answer it. It was Mrs. Korman.

"Hi!" I said. "Your house is fine. Did you get our message?"

Guess what! The Kormans said I could have the picnic at their pool. Yes!

I told my family my idea.

"We would like to have our own barbecue in the evening," said Daddy. "But an afternoon picnic with your friends sounds like a great idea."

Nannie offered to help me plan it.

"I want to send invitations!" I said. "I will need five of them. My guests will be Hannie, Nancy, Terri, Tammy, and Kristin. I will make the invitations red, white, and blue in honor of the Fourth of July."

"What kind of food do you want to serve?" asked Nannie.

"Sandwiches and chips and soda," I said.

"How about watermelon?" asked Nannie.

"Good idea."

"And would you like some homemade candy? We can make red, white, and blue taffy."

"Your taffy is the best!" I replied.

Nannie has her own candy-making business. She works in our old pantry. Daddy turned it into a second kitchen for her. I am an excellent helper. (I once helped Nannie win the Cocoa-Best Chocolate Cook-off contest. She won big prizes.) I was excited about my party. I thought I might be sad at the end of June when swim team practice ended. But now I had something exciting to look forward to.

I ran upstairs to get started on my invitations.

Go, Team, Go!

The meet on Thursday was set for eight o'clock at our pool. The visiting team was Howard Township.

"I am so excited!" I said to Terri and Kristin.

"I am glad we practiced again this afternoon at the Kormans' pool," said Terri.

I had invited my friends over to the Kormans' for a premeet warm-up practice.

At seven-thirty the visiting team's bus pulled up to the Community Center and the swimmers piled out. We let them have the first cheer, because they were our guests. Then we followed with ours.

Two, four, six, eight,
We are Stoneybrook swimmers and we are
great!
We are Stoneybrook swimmers and we are
cool.
Better watch out when we jump in the pool!
Yea!

We spent the next fifteen minutes doing warm-ups and giving pep talks. Then, at eight o'clock sharp, Coach Carson's whistle blew.

"Welcome, everyone," he said. "Our first event is the eight and under fifty-meter freestyle. Swimmers, please take your places."

Our coach does not waste words. He gets right down to business. If I were coach, I would take longer welcoming our guests. I would wish everyone luck and tell them to

have a good time. But I was not coach and our meet was starting.

"Fifteen seconds!" called Coach Carson.

Then he blew the whistle and the swimmers dived in.

"Go, team, go!" Terri, Kristin, Jenna, and I cheered our team on. (Jenna was the other girl in our relay.) *"Two, four, six, eight! We are Stoneybrook swimmers and we are . . ."*

Oops. We lost the round.

"Hey, hey, that's okay. We'll win the meet anyway!" our team chanted.

But we did not win the next race either. The meet was not going very well.

"I hope Coach Carson is not angry," said Terri.

Our event was one of the last of the evening. By then our team had caught up and was almost tied. The pressure was on.

"Maybe I should switch to the butterfly stroke. I already have butterflies in my stomach," I said.

"You are doing freestyle," said Jenna. "I am doing the butterfly."

"I am glad I am doing the backstroke," said Kristin.

"I wish I did not have to do the breast-stroke," said Terri. "I am still not sure about the kick."

"Relay swimmers, take your places!" called our coach.

The whistle blew. Kristin started strong. But at the end of her second lap she was lagging behind.

The butterflies in my stomach were going wild. In a few seconds I would have to swim as fast as I could. The next thing I knew, Kristin's hand touched the wall and I was diving in.

I was so nervous that I was having trouble breathing. Water went up my nose. But I had to keep going. I had to move fast. I touched the wall and turned to finish my lap. I could hardly believe it. I was pulling ahead of the other team's swimmer! I was slicing through the water.

I made it to the wall and Jenna dived in. Jenna has a strong butterfly stroke. She widened our lead. It was Terri's turn.

"Go for it!" I called to Terri as she dived in.

Terri was doing the breaststroke much better than she had when she started with the team. But it was not fast enough. We lost our lead. We lost the relay. And we lost the meet by just a few points.

"Stoneybrook lost because I am not a good enough swimmer," said Terri. "Maybe I should not be on the team."

"Of course you should be on the team," said Kristin. "You did your personal best. You should be proud."

I kept quiet. I was gigundoly disappointed that we had lost. I decided I would just have to swim harder next time. If I swam harder, maybe we would win.

Coach Meanie-mo

On Friday morning I was standing with Terri and Kristin when Coach Carson walked over to us. He looked at Terri.

"Who taught you to do the breaststroke?" he asked.

Terri shrugged. "I do not remember. I may have learned in day camp two summers ago."

"You either forgot or were not taught very well," said the coach.

I did not like the way he was talking to

my friend. I felt like telling him he should have helped her more before our meet. Then maybe we would have won.

Coach Carson looked at his watch and said, "Wait right here."

It was nine o'clock sharp. Our coach never starts late. He blew the whistle.

"I want you to work out on your own for a few minutes," he said to the team. "I have a swimmer who needs instruction."

Terri turned pale.

"We will be right in the next lane," I told her.

Between warm-up laps, Kristin and I watched Coach teach Terri the breaststroke kick. He was not friendly about it, but he made sense.

A few minutes later, our practice began.

"We lost to Howard Township," said our coach. "But it was our first meet. I expect us to do better next time. In fact, I expect us to win. Fifteen seconds to a fifty-meter freestyle!"

He blew the whistle and I swam hard.

I had promised myself that I would try harder. I was keeping my promise.

When we finished the freestyle, Coach said, "Thirty seconds to a hundred-meter breaststroke." Terri gave me a worried look.

"Just do what Coach taught you," I said.

The whistle blew. I pushed off and started moving. When I lifted my head, I could see Coach Carson coming our way.

"Barkan, snap those legs together. Give it some muscle!" he called.

Poor Terri.

"No! You have it all wrong! Bring those legs up!" the coach called.

We were only on our first lap. There were three more to go. Coach Carson was barking at Terri with almost every stroke. Before she made the final turn, she started spluttering and stopped to hug the wall.

Our coach blew the end-of-the-round whistle for the other swimmers. Then he did something awful. He made everyone watch Terri do her final lap of breaststroke.

"Here is an example of the things you

should *not* be doing in the breaststroke. Look and learn," he said.

"I cannot believe how mean he is!" said Kristin. She said it quietly so Coach would not hear.

When Terri finally reached the wall, she looked as if she would burst into tears.

"Young lady, now that I have taught you the proper kick, I expect you to practice it. You will see what a difference it makes at the next meet," said the coach.

He talked to us about the meet, which was scheduled for Wednesday.

"These meets are about more than just swimming. They are about being a team player," he said. "To be a team player you need discipline. You need concentration. These are not magic potions. They are skills. Learn them. You will swim better. You will do everything better."

I knew he was right. Whenever I did something while I daydreamed, it came out wrong. When I thought about what I was doing, it came out better. Coach Carson was making sense again. But Terri did not care.

"I do not like our coach anymore. I do not like him one bit!" she said.

"He was very tough on you," said Kristin.

"He was a meanie-mo," I said. "But you have to admit he was right about the kick. And all those things he said about discipline and concentration were true too. I think you should give him another chance. He is only trying to help us."

Our rides were waiting for us when we got outside. I had not changed Terri's mind about Coach Carson. But my mind was made up. Coach Carson was only trying to help us be winners.

The Scolding

I woke up on Monday ready to work hard for my team.

At breakfast, I played a concentration game. I opened a cupboard and memorized the cans on the top shelf. Split-pea soup, jumbo cashew nuts, baby corn kernels, sweet peas. While I ate, I concentrated on the list.

"Hi, how is swimming going?" asked Sam when he came into the kitchen.

"I cannot talk now. I am doing something important for practice," I replied.

"Really? It looks to me like you are eating a bowl of Krispy Krunchie cereal," said Sam.

"I am concentrating. Coach Carson says we need to learn discipline and concentration to do well on the team," I said. "Now you made me forget a can!"

A few minutes later, Nannie drove me to practice. It started off well. We did our warm-ups. Then Coach gave us some tips on the freestyle. He showed us how to do an S-curve with our arms underwater.

"Bring your arms in, then push the water away!" he said. "I will come around and watch you work on this."

He started with the fastest swimmers. Boo. He always started with them. I used the extra time to practice.

I swam one lap, pulling the water in, then pushing it away. When I got back to the other end, Terri and Kristin were hanging on to the wall, laughing.

"What is so funny?" I asked.

"I did not hear right and I was trying to do an X-curve!" said Terri.

"It looked so funny!" said Kristin. "I think we should do a B-curve. Bzzz."

I was hanging on to the wall laughing with my friends. I did not see Coach Carson coming our way.

"Girls, get back to your swimming immediately," he said.

"But I already did two — "

I wanted to tell the coach that I had done two laps. But he had already turned and walked away.

Boo and bullfrogs. I had been having such a good morning. I had done my concentration exercises. I had done two laps very well with the S-curve. I was trying hard.

Terri, Kristin, and I were careful not to talk during the rest of the practice. At the end, Coach Carson asked to speak to us.

"I am not happy with your attitude," he said. "This swim team is not meant to be fun and games. Did any of you hear a word I said yesterday about discipline and concentration?"

"I heard and I — "

I tried to explain how hard I was trying. But the coach would not listen.

"If you want to spend your summer giggling, find somewhere else to go. This pool, during swim team practice, is not the place. Is that understood?"

None of us said a word. We just nodded.

When we reached the locker room, Terri said, "He is so mean!"

"You are right," said Kristin. "He is awful!"

"I think he could say things a little more nicely. But I do not blame him for being angry," I said. "We should not waste time fooling around when we could be practicing. How can we win at the meets if we do not practice?"

"Winning does not matter so much. He should not be mean," said Terri.

I felt bad that my friends were so upset. But as the coach said, swim team practices were not all fun and games.

I wanted to win. I was going to try my best.

Coach Karen

I was not the only one trying my best at swimming. Emily was trying hard too.

On Monday after practice, Daddy, Emily, and I headed to the Kormans' pool.

"I hope the Kormans are having fun on their vacation," I said. "I am having a lot of fun in their pool."

"And I think Emily is going to learn to swim this summer," said Daddy.

"Emmie go in the water!" said my sister when we reached the Kormans'.

"I think you are ready to see how it feels

without your water wings," said Daddy.

Daddy and I walked Emily down the steps in the shallow end. Then Daddy took both of Emily's hands in his and let her kick around.

"Wheee!" said Emily as Daddy pulled her along.

I was supposed to be practicing my breaststroke, but Daddy and Emily were having so much fun.

"May I have a turn holding Emily?" I asked.

Daddy did not look too sure.

"I will not let her go even for a second," I said.

"Emily, Karen is going to swim with you for awhile," said Daddy.

I took Emily's hands and pulled her around the way Daddy had. Emily kicked happily. Daddy sat at the edge of the pool watching us.

"I think Emily should see how it feels to put her face in the water," I said. "She can blow bubbles."

"That is just how I taught you," said Daddy. "You show Emily how."

I pulled Emily near the steps and stood by her side.

"Okay, Emily, watch me," I said.

I put my face into the water and blew.

"Bubbles!" said Emily.

"Now you try it," I said.

Emily put her face in the water. Then her whole head followed. She came up spluttering.

"No, just put your face in," I said.

Emily tried again. This time she put just her face in.

"Now blow bubbles," I said.

Emily blew hard. In a couple of seconds she came up spluttering again. She did not look happy.

"You are blowing too hard," I said. "Blow lightly. Like this."

I showed Emily how. She tried again. But she blew just as hard as before.

"No, that is all wrong!" I said. "You have to concentrate!"

I guess I said it pretty loudly. Emily burst into tears. Daddy slipped into the water and scooped her up in his arms.

"Why are you being so hard on Emily? She is doing her best," said Daddy.

"I am sorry I made her cry. I was trying to help her the way Coach Carson helps us at practice," I said. "I want to help her swim to win."

"This is not the swim team," said Daddy. "We are trying to help your sister feel at home in the water. Shouting is not the way."

"I am sorry, Emily," I said. "Will you let me try again?"

"No!" said Emily.

I did not blame her. I left Emily with Daddy and practiced my stroke.

Flip Turns

The next morning at practice, Coach Carson taught us something new and exciting. Flip turns.

"There are four steps to a flip turn," he said. "The approach. The tuck. The flip. The push-off."

The coach worked with us for a long time. He was not mean. He was just very clear about how we should do a flip turn. I thought that was a good thing.

"The flip turn can make a big difference in

your race. Learn it. Practice it. Use it," he said.

The hardest part for me was still getting to the wall at the right time. A couple of times I hit the heels of my feet on the wall. That hurt! Then other times, I missed the wall completely. Finally I got the hang of it. The rest of the swimmers in my group were giving up.

"It is too much like diving," said Kristin. "I do not like being head down in the water."

"I cannot do it at all," said Terri. "Flipping makes me mixed up and dizzy."

I practiced the turn in the Kormans' pool two days in a row. Our next meet was a very important one. It was our second meet with Howard Township. We had lost the first meet. This was our chance to win!

I practiced hard. When it was time for the meet, I was ready for it. I was sure that doing the flip turns the way Coach Carson taught me was going to make all the difference.

This time we were the visiting team. We chanted our team cheer so loudly that we probably woke their whole town.

It was not long before the meet began. I was in two races. Freestyle and backstroke. As soon as I hit the water, my teammates shouted, "Go, Karen, go! Go, Karen, go!"

I felt like a world-famous sports star. The only things missing were the TV cameras and sports announcers. I swam as hard as I could.

Guess what! I took second place and third. Of course I wished I had been first. But the points from my races helped put us over the top and we won the meet! We *won* it!

"Good job, Brewer," said Coach Carson when I got on the bus to go home.

Good job? Was that all? He did not sound very excited, considering how well I had done.

"I got us a lot of points," I said. "I helped us win!"

"Yes. Maybe one day you will take first

place," said the coach. "Okay, now move to the back of the bus. You are holding up the other swimmers."

I stomped down the aisle and threw myself onto a seat. My coach was a big meanie-mo. I was the only kid my age doing flip turns and he *still* was not happy. Boo and bullfrogs. I was not happy either.

On Thursday morning, Coach Carson said, "I have a swimmer who needs instruction."

I felt sorry for the swimmer. I hoped it was not Terri. She was already feeling upset about our meet because she had not done very well.

Everyone turned to see who Coach Carson was going to work with. He walked toward our lane. Uh-oh. Poor Terri.

"Karen Brewer, we need to work on your turns," he said.

I could not believe my ears.

"The rest of you, get busy doing warm-ups," said the coach.

"I thought my turns were pretty good," I said to him when he turned back to me.

"I am not here to talk. I came to watch you swim. Flip!" said Coach Carson.

I looked at his face. I could see that this was no time to argue. I swam away from the wall. Then I swam back and flipped. The coach asked me to do it again. And again. And again. He gave me pointers each time. I was glad for the pointers. My turns were getting better. But I was also getting dizzy.

"Is it okay if I take a little break?" I asked.

"No, it is not. If you want to be a winner, you have to be strong," said Coach Carson. "Remember to take a big bite of air before you turn. Let me see it again."

I had to do it. After all, he was our coach. But I did not like it. I was dizzy and tired. Finally I saw what Terri was talking about. Our coach was mean. He barked his orders at us. I do not even know if he was happy when I got points at the swim meet. It felt like nothing we did could please him.

If being on the team meant being treated like this, maybe I did not want to be on it at all.

Red, White, and Blue

I was glad I was not going to the Kormans' pool in the afternoon. I had done enough swimming for one day.

I had invited Terri and Kristin over to make Fourth of July decorations and plan our menu.

"We should make Fourth of July Popsicles!" I said. "We can make red, white, and blue ones."

"Great idea," said Terri. "They can be cherry, lemon, and blueberry."

"We can have a No-Drip Contest," said Kristin. "Each player gets a point for every drip. Whoever has the least points is the winner."

We were coming up with excellent ideas. I needed to write them down. I found a sheet of paper and wrote *Menu* at the top. Below that I wrote *Popsicles — red, white, and blue.* At the top of another page I wrote *Games.* Below that I wrote *No-Drip Contest.*

"I think Coach Carson is a drip," said Terri. "All he thinks about is winning."

"He is so hard on us," said Kristin. "I am not so sure I want to stay on his team."

"But it is *our* team. It is fun being together and I like swimming," I said. "At least I used too. Coach Carson is kind of taking the fun out of it."

"He sure is," said Terri. "I used to like swimming too, even though I am not so good at it."

"I do not want to talk about the coach now," said Kristin. "I want to talk about the

Fourth of July. I think we should make American flags."

"Good idea," I said. "We can make the flags right now!"

I got out red, white, and blue construction paper.

"We each need to make two flags," I said. "Ones for ourselves and ones for Tammy, Hannie, and Nancy."

I wondered how Hannie and Nancy were doing. Even though I was having fun with my new summer friends, I missed my old ones.

"I would like to have watermelon at the picnic," said Terry. "And I would like to know what we should do about Coach Carson. I know we do not want to talk about him too much. But I cannot help it. He is on my mind."

"That is okay," said Kristin. "I cannot help thinking about him either."

"Getting watermelon for the picnic is easy," I said. "Figuring out what to do about Coach Carson is hard. I think this is too hard

to figure out by ourselves. We have to ask our parents for help."

"I think you are right," said Terri.

We made our flags and added some more food and games to our list. We did a good day's work.

After Terri and Kristin left, I talked to Daddy and Elizabeth. I told them all about Coach Carson.

"I cannot believe it is the same Ron Carson we have read about," said Elizabeth. "He is a town hero."

"He is also a meanie-mo," I replied.

I told them how he scolded Terri when she could not do the breaststroke kick the right way. And I told them that he had not been nice to me when I got on the bus. "That was after I did flip turns and helped get points for our team," I said.

I told them how he made me do flip turns till I was dizzy.

"I am glad you are telling us these things, Karen," said Daddy. "When we come to your meet tomorrow night we will be sure to keep our eyes on Coach Carson. Then we will have a better idea what to do."

My troubles were not over. I still had to go to practice in the morning. But help was on the way.

Mr. Nice Coach

Friday morning practice was no fun. Coach Carson was his meanie-mo self. He pushed too hard and talked too much about winning. I hoped our plan to get grown-up help was going to work.

Our meet that night was held at our pool. We were competing against the Rockville swim team. Coach Carson blew the whistle to get our attention.

"Greetings and welcome to Stoneybrook," he said. "Stoneybrook swimmers, we need a big welcoming cheer for our guests."

Two, four, six, eight!
Who do we appreciate?
Rockville swim team!
Rockville swim team! Yea!

Kristin, Terri, and I were standing near the pool with our team. We were cheering as loudly as we could. I waved to my family seated above us.

"And now let the swimming begin!" said Coach Carson.

He was acting very friendly and nice. I wondered when he would change into his mean self.

My first race was the fifty-meter freestyle. I came in third.

"Watch him change now," I said to Kristin and Terri.

Guess what. He was nice, even though I had not won the race.

"Good job, Karen," he said. "Your flip turn has improved."

"Thank you," I replied.

Wow! I did not remember the coach saying two nice sentences in a row before. I decided to enjoy the coach while he was on good behavior.

The scores were close until the end of the meet. Then Stoneybrook pulled ahead. My friends and I cheered so loudly that our throats hurt.

On the way home, Daddy said, "We believe what you and your friends told us about Coach Carson. But he seemed fine tonight."

"We will need to see for ourselves what he is doing wrong before we can decide what to do," said Elizabeth.

"You will have another chance to see him in action on Monday," I replied. "We are going to Rockville for a second meet."

"We will drive as many of your team members as we can to the meet," said Daddy. "And we will invite your coach to join us. Maybe we can get a better idea what he is like in closer quarters."

But on Monday at the meet, Coach was just as nice. He had even been nice at our practice that morning. For the first time, he gave us a demonstration. He wanted to show us that we did not have to lift our heads much when we turned to breathe during the freestyle.

It was exciting to watch a famous swimmer dive into the pool right in front of us. He hardly even splashed. Then he swam across the pool. He made it look easy, but I had never seen anyone go so fast.

Boo. Our coach was being too nice. I had never thought I would wish for a person to be mean. I needed Daddy and Elizabeth to see for themselves what I was talking about. But Coach Carson would not cooperate.

At the meet that night he led our cheers. He gave us last-minute pointers about our strokes. And when the Rockville team wanted pictures of the visiting star, he posed for them. He was friendly the whole time.

The coach's good mood did not help our swimming, though. We lost to Rockville by just a few points.

"Now Daddy and Elizabeth will see his true self," I whispered to Kristin and Terri.

But I was wrong. The coach said we should all try harder next time. That was all. Everyone, including the coach, was quiet on the ride home.

I wondered if Daddy and Elizabeth would ever get to see him when he was being mean. Maybe he was just mean to kids when he was alone with them. Maybe he was ashamed of himself for being mean and was afraid to let other grown-ups see.

I needed a plan. I am very good at making plans. But I could come up with only one idea. My idea was to do something very bad in front of the coach while Daddy and Elizabeth were watching. Then they would see him be mean to me. But it was not a very good plan. I would probably end up in more trouble than the coach.

I had made it through two weeks of the swim team. I could make it through two more.

Racing Dives

Tuesday was chilly and gray.

"You do not have to go to practice today if you do not want to," said Elizabeth.

"Maybe it would be good for you to take a day off, since you have been having problems with Coach Carson," said Daddy.

"That is okay," I replied. "I want to go. Even if the coach is a meanie-mo, he is still right about some things. He says we should stick to our routines. And that is a good idea."

"I am proud of you, Karen," said Daddy.

"You are being very grown-up in a difficult situation."

That was a nice thing to hear. I felt gigundoly proud of myself.

Daddy dropped me off in front of the Community Center and I met my friends at the pool. Our coach did not look happy.

"I failed to teach you something important," he said. "I should have had you all working on this from the start. You need to work on your racing dives. Racing dives can turn you into winners."

I heard Kristin gasp.

"Racing dives give you your fastest start. A good dive will put you halfway across the pool before you come up for air," he said. "I want everyone on this team to learn this dive and learn it well."

"I cannot do it!" whispered Kristin. "I will have to quit the team."

"Do not quit yet," I replied. "Maybe if you watch the other kids doing the dives, you will not be so scared."

As usual, Coach Carson started helping

the best swimmers first. He asked the rest of us to watch.

He told the kids to climb up onto the starting blocks. I could see some of them shivering in the chilly morning air. They listened to the coach's instructions. Then he blew the whistle.

They all dove into the water. Only a couple of kids made it even a quarter of the way across the pool.

"That was pitiful!" said the coach. "Back on the blocks."

The kids got out of the water and climbed back up on the blocks. They listened to the coach explain what they had done wrong. I could see them shivering harder than before. One girl's teeth were chattering.

"I cannot do this," whispered Kristin again.

"Keep watching," I said.

Coach made the same kids dive in the water then climb back onto the blocks five times in a row. By the fifth time on the blocks, their lips had turned blue.

"It is too cold," said Terri quietly. "He needs to cancel the practice. If we get sick, he will not have any swimmers at the next meet."

But the coach was not about to cancel practice. No way. He was headed in our direction.

I looked at Kristin. She was shaking like a leaf. I did not think it was because of the cold. We were still dry, and she was wearing a sweatshirt. Kristin was shaking with fear.

Rescued!

"Up on the blocks!" said Coach Carson.

I took off my T-shirt and stepped forward. Kristin was not the only one shaking. Terri and I were both shaking now too.

If I was going to dive off the block, I needed someone to show me patiently how to do it. I had trouble understanding when the coach barked orders at us.

But I did not think I had a choice. Neither did Kristin nor Terri. We climbed onto our blocks.

I had never been on a block before. It felt

awfully high up. I glanced down into the pool. It looked cold, dark, and far away.

"Fifteen seconds to go," said Coach Carson.

I was trying to decide whether I actually had to go through with the dive when I heard my name being called. I turned and saw Daddy and Mr. Barkan walking toward us.

"Daddy!" I shouted.

My friends and I jumped down from the blocks and ran to Daddy and Terri's father.

"What are you doing here?" I asked.

"We decided to stay and watch practice for awhile," Daddy replied. "This looked like the right time to ask Mr. Carson a few questions."

"Thank you!" said Kristin.

I had never seen anyone look so relieved. The five of us walked to Coach Carson together.

"Coach, these kids look awfully unhappy to me," said Daddy. "Can you tell us what is going on?"

"I am trying to teach them some winning

strategies, Mr. Brewer," replied the coach. "You saw how they lost the meet last night. You were there."

"But it is a very chilly day. Look at these kids. They are shivering," said Mr. Barkan.

"I cannot do anything about the weather. But I can do something to help them win our next meet."

"This might be a good day to do land exercise and instruction," said Mr. Barkan. "Or you might consider canceling practice altogether."

"Canceling does not make winners," said Coach Carson.

"These kids just want to enjoy a summer swim program. They are not trying out for the Olympics," said Daddy. "Why is winning so important?"

Coach Carson just stood there. He had no answer for Daddy. He looked at the faces of all the kids who had gathered around.

"I am sorry," he said. "I will go see the program director. I am sure someone will be out to speak with you soon."

Apologies

It had started raining. So we went inside the Community Center and waited for someone to come speak with us.

Finally Mrs. Barton, the program director, appeared.

"Good morning, everyone," she said. "I am sorry about this miserable weather."

Mrs. Barton smiled. She is a very nice person.

"I have spoken with Mr. Carson and he explained what happened this morning," said Mrs. Barton. "I think this brings to light a situation that needs correction. Mr. Carson has resigned as coach of the swim team."

The kids all started talking at once. This had been a bad day. But no one expected the coach to resign. I had a feeling that Daddy and Mr. Barkan were not the first parents to talk with Coach Carson.

"If you will give me a minute more, I will explain why," said Mrs. Barton.

Everyone settled down to listen.

"As you know, Mr. Carson has been a winning athlete for much of his life," said Mrs. Barton. "Part of his enjoyment of swimming comes from competing and winning. Unfortunately, Mr. Carson's goals and the goals of the Community Center were not the same. He expected to create a winning swim team. All we wanted to offer was a summer program children could learn from and enjoy. This situation became a great frustration to Mr. Carson and we understand that some of his frustration was taken out on you. For that we are all sorry. And now I believe Mr. Carson has something to say."

She waved to Coach Carson, who was waiting inside. I felt confused. I did not like the way Coach Carson had been treating us. Today I had even felt a little scared of him. But he was our coach. I could still see that he was trying to do what he thought was best for us. I would have liked winning medals. (They would have looked gigundoly good in my room!) But I wanted to have fun swimming with my friends more than I wanted medals. And I definitely did not like being scolded when I was really and truly trying my best.

Then Mr. Carson came into the room and stood in front of us.

"I will be brief," he said. "First of all, I am sorry if I made any of you kids uncomfortable. I meant to help, not hurt you. I see I was not very good at it. I hope that in these couple of weeks at least a few of you have learned to swim a little better. I learned a lot about myself from this experience. Maybe my skills and goals are better suited to coaching older kids. Enjoy the rest of your summer vacation. And keep swimming!"

Mr. Carson walked away quickly. Mrs. Barton told us that she would try to find another swim coach as soon as possible.

"It may take a little time to find a coach. But we will hire an extra lifeguard immediately and the pool will open during swim team hours for recreational swimming."

That was it. Coach Carson was gone. I gave Daddy a hug. Then my friends and I linked arms and headed outside.

Happy Fourth of July!

When I woke up on Wednesday morning, I felt lost. For weeks I had been waking up in time for practice. Now there was none.

My friends and I had decided to take the day off from the Community Center. (Terri's mom was dropping her off at Kristin's aunt's house on her way to work.) It was not a day for swimming anyway. It was chilly and gray again.

I thought about curling up under the covers and going back to sleep. Then I remembered something else I had to look forward to. The Fourth of July! I hopped out of bed and ran downstairs.

"You are up early," said Nannie.

"I have things to do!" I said. "I mean, *we* have things to do. Can we start making candy for the picnic?"

"We certainly can," said Nannie. "Would you like to invite your friends to come help us?"

"Sure!" I replied.

I ate breakfast, then called Kristin's aunt's house. I invited Kristin and Terri to come for lunch and candy-making.

The rest of June passed in a blur. Before I knew it, it was the Fourth of July and I was hosting our picnic at the Kormans' pool. My guests were Hannie, Nancy, Kristin, Terri, and Tammy. Nannie, Emily, and Daddy were there too. We were having our dessert.

"Pass the taffy, please," said Hannie.

"Red, white, or blue?" I asked.

"One of each!" replied Hannie.

Hannie and Nancy already knew Terri

and Tammy from school. And they were glad to meet Kristin. They liked her a lot. I was happy all my friends were getting along so well.

"This taffy is delicious!" said Hannie.

"Do not get too full. We have one more surprise dessert," I said.

I ran into the Kormans' house. Nannie and I had put the Popsicles in the freezer.

"Ta-daa!" I said when I returned with a tray of them. I explained the No-Drip Contest rules to Hannie and Nancy. Guess who won. Me!

Later, when our stomachs had settled down after our meal, we got into the pool.

"Who wants to race?" I asked.

"Um, what stroke will we be doing?" asked Kristin.

"We will do your favorite. The backstroke!" I replied.

"Thank goodness you did not say breaststroke," said Terri. "I still cannot get that kick right."

I raced hard, but lost. Hannie was the winner.

"You are a good swimmer," said Kristin.

"I swam almost every day on my vacation," Hannie replied. "My mom loves to swim. She taught me the strokes."

"I am sure she did not bark orders at you like our coach did," I said.

It was the best picnic. After my friends left and my family and I had cleaned up, I got back into the pool.

"Emily, do you want to try blowing bubbles again?" I asked.

My sister looked worried. Our first try had not gone very well. But finally Emily said okay.

I made sure to be very patient. On her first few tries, Emily blew too hard. Then she hardly blew at all. I told her to think of the story about the Three Bears.

"You do not want to blow too hard. You do not want to blow too softly. You want to blow just right," I said.

After many more tries, Emily put her face in the water and blew one more time.

"You did it just right!" I said.

Emily's face lit up. I decided I might never make it to the Olympics as a swimmer. But maybe someday I could be a coach. Emily was my first student. And she and I were both doing very well.

L. GODWIN

About the Author

ANN M. MARTIN lives in New York City and loves animals, especially cats. She has two cats of her own, Gussie and Woody.

Other books by Ann M. Martin that you might enjoy are *Stage Fright; Me and Katie (the Pest);* and the books in *The Baby-sitters Club* series.

Ann likes ice cream and *I Love Lucy*. And she has her own little sister, whose name is Jane.

Don't miss #111

KAREN'S SPY MYSTERY

I decided to see what he was doing. I found my binoculars on my desk. Mommy had told me it was not polite to spy on people. But I had to make sure Nancy's house was okay. After all, I promised Nancy I would look after it.

I walked over to my window and focused the binoculars. The curtains in Nancy's house were open, so I could see a lot. And guess what? Bill Barnett was in Nancy's parents' bedroom, looking at their books. Once in a while he took a book off the shelf, opened it, then put it back on the shelf. He carried a red notebook with him. Then he sat on the bed to write in it. Was he making a list of the books in Nancy's house? Was he looking for something valuable?

Little Sister

by Ann M. Martin
author of The Baby-sitters Club®

More Titles... ➡

❑	MQ69188-0 #80	Karen's Christmas Tree	$2.99
❑	MQ69189-9 #81	Karen's Accident	$2.99
❑	MQ69190-2 #82	Karen's Secret Valentine	$3.50
❑	MQ69191-0 #83	Karen's Bunny	$3.50
❑	MQ69192-9 #84	Karen's Big Job	$3.50
❑	MQ69193-7 #85	Karen's Treasure	$3.50
❑	MQ69194-5 #86	Karen's Telephone Trouble	$3.50
❑	MQ06585-8 #87	Karen's Pony Camp	$3.50
❑	MQ06586-6 #88	Karen's Puppet Show	$3.50
❑	MQ06587-4 #89	Karen's Unicorn	$3.50
❑	MQ06588-2 #90	Karen's Haunted House	$3.50
❑	MQ06589-0 #91	Karen's Pilgrim	$3.50
❑	MQ06590-4 #92	Karen's Sleigh Ride	$3.50
❑	MQ06591-2 #93	Karen's Cooking Contest	$3.50
❑	MQ06592-0 #94	Karen's Snow Princess	$3.50
❑	MQ06593-9 #95	Karen's Promise	$3.50
❑	MQ06594-7 #96	Karen's Big Move	$3.50
❑	MQ06595-5 #97	Karen's Paper Route	$3.50
❑	MQ06596-3 #98	Karen's Fishing Trip	$3.50
❑	MQ49760-X #99	Karen's Big City Mystery	$3.50
❑	MQ50051-1 #100	Karen's Book	$3.50
❑	MQ50053-8 #101	Karen's Chain Letter	$3.50
❑	MQ50054-6 #102	Karen's Black Cat	$3.50
❑	MQ50055-4 #103	Karen's Movie Star	$3.99
❑	MQ50056-2 #104	Karen's Christmas Carol	$3.99
❑	MQ50057-0 #105	Karen's Nanny	$3.99
❑	MQ50058-9 #106	Karen's President	$3.99
❑	MQ50059-7 #107	Karen's Copycat	$3.99
❑	MQ43647-3	Karen's Wish Super Special #1	$3.25
❑	MQ44834-X	Karen's Plane Trip Super Special #2	$3.25
❑	MQ44827-7	Karen's Mystery Super Special #3	$3.25
❑	MQ45644-X	Karen, Hannie, and Nancy	
		The Three Musketeers Super Special #4	$2.95
❑	MQ45649-0	Karen's Baby Super Special #5	$3.50
❑	MQ46911-8	Karen's Campout Super Special #6	$3.25
❑	MQ55407-7	BSLS Jump Rope Pack	$5.99
❑	MQ73914-X	BSLS Playground Games Pack	$5.99
❑	MQ89735-7	BSLS Photo Scrapbook Book and Camera Pack	$9.99
❑	MQ47677-7	BSLS School Scrapbook	$2.95
❑	MQ13801-4	Baby-sitters Little Sister Laugh Pack	$6.99
❑	MQ26497-2	Karen's Summer Fill-In Book	$2.95

Available wherever you buy books, or use this order form.

Scholastic Inc., P.O. Box 7502, Jefferson City, MO 65102

Please send me the books I have checked above. I am enclosing $_____
(please add $2.00 to cover shipping and handling). Send check or money order – no
cash or C.O.Ds please.

Name_____ Birthdate_____

Address_____

City_____ State/Zip_____

Please allow four to six weeks for delivery. Offer good in U.S.A. only. Sorry, mail orders are not available to residents of Canada. Prices subject to change.   BSLS998